# The Crypt of Destiny

Donald A. Salerno Jr.

Cover & Illustrations: Donald A. Salerno Jr

(All images were generated with the assistance of AI DALL-E2)

"The Crypt of Destiny," by Donald A Salerno Jr. ISBN 978-1-63868-166-3 (softcover); 978-1-63868-167-0 (eBook).

Published 2024 by Virtualbookworm.com Publishing Inc., P.O. Box 9949, College Station, TX 77842, US. ©2024, Donald A. Salerno Jr. All rights reserved. No part of this publication may be reproduced, stored in a retrieval system, or transmitted in any form or by any means, electronic, mechanical, recording or otherwise, without the prior written permission of Donald A. Salerno Jr, except for brief quotations in critical reviews or articles.

# Table of Contents

# Background

In the year 2180, humanity's greatest technological advancements have ironically heralded its downfall. A groundbreaking geneticist, Cirus Ptak, earlier in the century, achieved a controversial feat by cloning Adolf Hitler, resulting in a clone named Histler VonMalmsteen. This clone, surpassing the infamy of Hitler, utilized his understanding of past mistakes to form a formidable alliance known as the Aryan Alliance, comprising China and the Muslim Republic of Iran. Leveraging China's vast resources and Iran's nuclear capabilities, combined with VonMalmsteen's strategic acumen, this alliance quickly subdued both Eastern and Western democracies.

The survivors of the ensuing war and nuclear fallout found themselves under the oppressive rule of VonMalmsteen, who crowned himself as the Grand Viceroy and 12th Imam of this newly established Empire. The empire, a fusion of radical Islam and Marxist socialism, exerted a level of control and suppression unprecedented in history. In this regime, all symbols and instruments of democracy and past capitalist societies were eradicated, leaving a generation utterly oblivious to the concepts of popular music, the internet, toys, digital media, comic books, and video games - the pillars of the pre-Empire technological era. Life under VonMalmsteen's rule was colorless and oppressive, with people resigned to a mundane existence of total subservience.

However, a glimmer of hope existed in the 21st century through the actions of a supreme covert operative, Dialus Mirpin. Involved in a top-secret wormhole experiment, Mirpin's consciousness was propelled into the future, giving him a glimpse of this grim reality. Realizing the futility of altering the future from the past, he devised a long-term plan to dismantle VonMalmsteen's empire. This plan centered around Kevin Piech, an ordinary individual with a collection of 21st-century artifacts. Mirpin, in a strategic move, befriended Piech and subtly influenced him to deposit his genetic material in a DNA bank and secure his collection in a crypt, locked with a nearly impenetrable DNA lock.

Upon Mirpin's death, his will specified that a key to a safe box containing his plan be sent through the wormhole to Dr. Xander Farrin, a colleague and rival of Ptak, who harbored a deep-seated grudge after Ptak stole his cloning research. Farrin, an overlooked scientist for VonMalmsteen's regime dreamed of greatness. Driven by revenge, Farrin followed Mirpin's instructions and extracted Piech's preserved DNA. In a clandestine laboratory, he created an exact clone of Piech, named Mortimer Braxton Piech. In his rage Farrin failed to discern his efforts were covertly guided by the very hands VonMalmsteen himself.

Mortimer, trained in secrecy amidst the backdrop of the war and the rise of VonMalmsteen's Empire, emerged as the most pivotal figure in human history.

He was the sole person possessing the unique DNA necessary to unlock the crypt containing Piech's collection – a key to potentially overthrowing VonMalmsteen's regime. This crypt, sealed by the unbreakable DNA lock, held more than just relics; it contained the essence of a lost era and possibly the means to ignite a revolution.

Thus began the extraordinary journey of Mortimer Braxton Piech, an obscure figure destined to be the linchpin in the fight against the Empire's tyranny. His mission, fraught with danger and shrouded in mystery, represented humanity's last hope to reclaim its past and forge a new future. This marks the beginning of our story...

# Chapter 1: Mortimer's Awakening

In the year 2180, under the oppressive regime of the Aryan Alliance, Mortimer Braxton Piech navigated the shadowed alleys of a city that had long forgotten the taste of freedom. The towering structures around him stood like silent sentinels, their surfaces cold and unyielding. It was a city frozen in time; its spirit crushed by the weight of authoritarian rule.

Mortimer's footsteps echoed on the cobblestone streets, a solitary sound in the otherwise muted world. He moved with purpose; his every step calculated to avoid the ever-watchful eyes of the regime's enforcers. His heart beat in tandem with the lurking dangers of the city, a constant reminder of the perilous life he led as a covert operative in the rebellion.

As Mortimer entered his modest apartment, the dim light from the flickering bulb cast long shadows across the room. The walls were adorned with mandatory propaganda posters of Histler VonMalmsteen, the tyrant who had reshaped the world in his diabolical vision. Mortimer's gaze lingered on the posters, each one a stark reminder of the world's descent into tyranny.

The room, much like the city itself, was a relic of a forgotten time - a place of stark simplicity and suppressed history. Mortimer's dinner, a tasteless ration provided by the regime, sat untouched on the table. The regime controlled everything, even sustenance, leaving the people with mere remnants of their former lives.

Yet, beneath the surface of compliance, Mortimer harbored a secret. He was part of a dwindling group of rebels, a band of individuals who clung to the memories of a world that once celebrated diversity, freedom, and creativity. In the quiet of his apartment, Mortimer allowed himself to remember - to dream of laughter, colors, and the voices of dissent that once filled the air.

That night, as Mortimer settled into a restless sleep, he was haunted by dreams of a different life - visions of a past that felt both familiar and distant. These dreams, echoes of a time before the Aryan Alliance's iron grip, whispered of a hidden truth, a reality buried beneath years of oppressive rule.

Unbeknownst to Mortimer, his role in the grand scheme of things was about to change. The dreams that night were more than mere figments of his imagination; they were a foreshadowing of an awakening that would shake the very foundations of the regime.

As the city slept, Mortimer's mind raced, caught in the turmoil of his dreams. He was on the cusp of a revelation, one that would not only alter his perception of the world but also set him on a path that would intersect with the fate of the rebellion.

In the shadows of his room, as the flickering bulb cast its dim light, Mortimer stood at the threshold of a journey that would lead him through the darkest corners of the regime and into the heart of a mystery that had shrouded his existence. The awakening of Mortimer Braxton Piech was just beginning.

# Chapter 2: Discovery of His Origins

The night wrapped the city in its quiet embrace as Mortimer lay awake, pondering the vivid dreams that seemed more like memories than figments of his imagination. The room felt smaller in the dark, the walls holding secrets of a past Mortimer were just beginning to unravel. The soft glow of the moonlight filtered through the curtains, casting eerie shadows that danced across the room.

A soft knock at the door jolted him from his thoughts. Cautiously, Mortimer approached. It was Varian, his face etched with urgency. "We need to talk," he whispered, slipping inside, his presence barely noticeable in the dimly lit room.

Mortimer's heart quickened at the solemn expression on Varian's face. "What's happened?" he asked, sensing the gravity in Varian's voice.

"It's about you, Mortimer," Varian replied, his voice barely above a breath. He glanced around the room as if checking for eavesdroppers, then continued, "We've uncovered something... about your origins."

Mortimer felt a chill run down his spine. "My origins? What are you talking about?"

Varian took a deep breath, his eyes locked onto Mortimer's. "Our intel suggests you might be more than just a rebel. There's evidence that you were part of VonMalmsteen's experiments – a product of his genetic manipulation."

The revelation hit Mortimer like a tidal wave, leaving him momentarily speechless. He had always felt a disconnect from his past, a piece of his history missing or altered. "Are you saying I'm not... I'm not who I think I am?"

"It appears so," Varian replied solemnly. "Your existence might be intertwined with the regime more than we ever suspected."

Mortimer's mind raced. He recalled flashes of his dreams – the strange familiarity with the regime's inner workings, the unexplainable knowledge of hidden passages and secrets. "What does this mean for us, for the rebellion?"

Varian placed a hand on Mortimer's shoulder, offering both comfort and resolve. "It means we tread carefully. But it also means you might have access to information we need. You could be the key to bringing down VonMalmsteen."

The weight of the revelation hung heavily in the air, like a storm cloud threatening to unleash its fury. Mortimer felt torn between the life he had known and the shadowy truth of his existence. "I need to understand more. I need to know who I truly am."

Varian nodded in agreement. "We'll do this together, Mortimer. We'll uncover your past and use it to shape our future. The regime may have created you for their purpose, but now, you have the power to dismantle it."

The night grew deeper as Mortimer and Varian plotted their next move. The city, asleep under the regime's watchful eye, was unaware of the storm brewing within its walls. Mortimer Braxton Piech, once a mere rebel, now stood at the heart of a revelation that could change the course of their struggle.

In the silence of the room, a new determination settled within Mortimer. His origins, shrouded in mystery and manipulation, would not define him. He would forge his own path, one that led towards freedom and truth. The night continued its silent vigil, unaware that within the darkness, the seeds of rebellion had just found fertile ground to grow.

# Chapter 3: Secrets Unveiled

Selene, a top rebel operative crouched low on the rooftop, hidden in the cover of the night. Her nimble fingers adjusted the focus on her binoculars as she scanned the grand building below. It was the heart of the regime's operations, the very lair of the oppressive ruler, Histler VonMalmsteen.

She had received a tip from a reliable source within the rebellion that VonMalmsteen was meeting with a high-ranking official, Xander

Farrin, in a private chamber tonight. The content of their conversation was rumored to be of utmost importance to the regime's agenda.

Selene was determined to uncover their secrets and gain any advantage for the rebellion. She knew this mission was risky, but the potential gains were worth the peril.

The night was moonless, shrouding the building in darkness. Selene wore a black, form-fitting suit that allowed her to blend seamlessly with the shadows. Her training as a covert operative in the rebellion had honed her skills in stealth and observation.

She waited patiently; her trained eyes focused on the building's balcony. Finally, the massive doors to the chamber swung open, and two figures stepped out. Selene's heart raced as she recognized VonMalmsteen, his cruel visage illuminated by the soft glow of the chamber's interior. Beside him was Xander Farrin, a man known for his cunning and ruthlessness.

Selene adjusted her binoculars, zooming in on the two men as they began to speak.

VonMalmsteen's voice was cold and calculated. "Farrin, you understand the importance of our plan. The rebel leader, Mortimer, is not who he appears to be. He carries a unique genetic marker that makes him the key to our ultimate goal."

Farrin's brows furrowed in curiosity. "What do you mean, VonMalmsteen?"

VonMalmsteen continued, his eyes narrowing. "Mortimer Braxton Piech is not just a random rebel. His DNA holds the key to unlocking the full potential of the Artifact"

Selene's heart skipped a beat. She had heard whispers of the Artifact—a mysterious technology rumored to have the power to reshape reality itself. If VonMalmsteen and Farrin intended to harness its power, it could spell disaster for the rebellion.

Farrin seemed intrigued but cautious. "And how do we plan to use him?"

VonMalmsteen's lips curled into a sinister smile. "We will lure Mortimer into a false sense of security. We'll feed him information about his family, his heritage. Once he believes he has the upper hand, we will strike. He will lead us right to the rebellion's core, and we will crush them once and for all."

Selene's mind raced. Mortimer had always been a mystery, even to the rebels. To learn that he held the key to the Artifact was a revelation that could change everything. But it also meant that he was in grave danger.

Farrin seemed to mull over the plan. "And what if he realizes he can access the Artifact?"

VonMalmsteen nodded, satisfaction evident in his voice. "Don't be concerned by the time he realizes the truth; it will be too late."

Selene's grip on her binoculars tightened. She needed to find a way to warn Mortimer and the rebellion about this impending trap. The information she had gathered tonight was invaluable, but it came at a great risk.

The conversation between VonMalmsteen and Farrin continued, delving into further details of their sinister plan. Selene remained hidden, her thoughts racing as she contemplated her next move.

As the two men retreated back into the chamber, Selene knew that the battle for Mortimer's destiny had reached a critical juncture. The secrets she had uncovered would be the key to averting disaster and protecting the rebellion.

# Chapter 4: Allies and Adversaries

As dawn broke over the city, casting a pale light on its somber streets, Mortimer and Varian ventured into the heart of the rebellion's secret haven. The air was thick with tension, a reflection of the uncertainty that Mortimer's revelations had brought. The rebellion's sanctuary, hidden beneath the city's façade of oppression, was a labyrinth of passages and chambers, a testament to the resilience of those who had dared to defy the regime.

In the dimly lit meeting chamber, faces turned towards them — a tapestry of hope, fear, and resolve. Varian stepped forward, addressing the assembly. "We stand at a crossroads," he began, his voice firm. "The regime's downfall may rest with one of our own. Mortimer's origins, though unsettling, could be the key to our victory."

Whispers filled the room. Mortimer felt the weight of every gaze upon him, the burden of his newfound identity pressing down. He knew the importance of this moment, the need to unite the fragmented whispers of doubt into a chorus of rebellion.

Selene, emerging from the shadows, spoke up, her voice laced with concern. "We can't ignore the risk," she said, her words echoing the unspoken doubts of many. "If Mortimer is indeed a creation of the regime, can we trust him? Can we risk the safety of our cause?"

Varian responded with conviction, "Distrust will only serve to divide us. We need to harness the potential Mortimer represents."

Mortimer, aware of the doubts and questions swirling around him, stepped forward. He felt a surge of resolve, a determination to prove his loyalty. "I may not know the full truth of my past, but I stand with you against VonMalmsteen's tyranny. My allegiance is to the rebellion, to our shared fight for freedom."

The room fell silent, each rebel pondering his words. It was Varian, the enigmatic strategist of their group, who broke the silence. "Let us use this revelation not as a wedge, but as a weapon. If Mortimer is connected to the regime, then we have an advantage. We must explore every possibility."

The discussion shifted, turning towards strategy and planning. Mortimer, now at the center of their cause, felt the gears of change turning. The meeting concluded with a renewed sense of purpose, a unified front against the regime.

But as the rebels dispersed, Mortimer's doubts lingered like a shadow. In a quiet corner, Selene approached him. Her eyes held a mixture of caution and concern. "I meant no offense earlier," she said softly. "But we must tread carefully. The regime is cunning, and we must be prepared for any eventuality."

Mortimer nodded, understanding the weight of her words. "I agree. We need to be vigilant and cautious. But I assure you, my fight is for our freedom, not for the regime's designs."

As Mortimer and Selene conversed, whispers of a potential traitor among the rebels reached their ears. The possibility sent a ripple of unease through the group. The battle against the regime was challenging enough, but facing an enemy within their ranks was a threat they had not anticipated.

Mortimer stood at the window, looking out at the city that had become both his prison and his battlefield. He knew the path ahead would be fraught with challenges, both external and internal. But his resolve was unshaken. The fight for freedom, for truth, was just beginning.

The days that followed were filled with intense training and meticulous planning. Mortimer's role within the rebellion had shifted, and he embraced it with unwavering determination. He honed his skills, delved into the intricacies of the regime's infrastructure, and sought to uncover any hidden knowledge that might aid their cause.

Varian, always the strategist, worked closely with Mortimer. "Your unique position could be our greatest advantage," he said one evening as they pored over maps and intelligence reports. "We need to exploit every opportunity to weaken VonMalmsteen's grip on the city."


Mortimer nodded, a sense of purpose driving him forward. Together, they formulated daring strategies, identifying vulnerable points in the regime's operations and planning covert operations to exploit them.

But beneath the surface, the undercurrent of distrust still flowed. Some rebels found it difficult to fully accept Mortimer, his origins a constant source of unease. Selene, ever vigilant, kept a watchful eye on him, her suspicion never fully abated.

One evening, in the dimly lit recesses of their hideout, Mortimer found himself alone with Selene. Her eyes bore into his, the weight of her scrutiny palpable. "You understand why I have to be cautious," she said, her voice soft but unwavering.

Mortimer met her gaze with equal determination. "I do. We can't afford to be complacent. If there's even a shred of doubt about my loyalty, it should be addressed."

Selene nodded, a hint of respect in her eyes. "You've proven yourself in the field, Mortimer. But we can't forget the stakes. The regime will stop at nothing to maintain its hold on power."

Their conversation served as a reminder of the delicate balance they had to maintain. Mortimer's loyalty to the rebellion was unquestionable, yet the shadows of his past still loomed, casting doubt on his every action.

# Chapter 5: Training and Preparation

The rebellion's hidden headquarters buzzed with activity, a stark contrast to the oppressive stillness of the city above. In this underground sanctuary, Mortimer found himself at the center of a whirlwind of preparation and strategy. The revelation of his origins had sparked a new urgency within the group, a need to act before the regime tightened its grip even further.

Varian took the lead in organizing the rebels. "We have a unique opportunity," he declared, addressing the gathered fighters. "Mortimer's connection to the regime, whether by fate or design, gives us an edge. We must be ready to strike when the time comes."

Training sessions were rigorous, testing the limits of each rebel. Mortimer participated with a fierce determination, driven by the need to prove his loyalty and the desperation to dismantle the world VonMalmsteen had created. Each grueling exercise, each strategy discussion, brought the rebels closer, forging them into a more cohesive unit.

Selene, always watchful, pulled Mortimer aside during a break. "Your training is progressing, but remember, the regime is not just an external enemy. The battle is also within, against the doubts and fears they've planted."

Mortimer nodded, grateful for her insight. "I know. I feel the conflict inside me every day. But I won't let it hold me back."

In the following days, Mortimer's role in the rebellion became more defined. His unique knowledge of the regime, though incomplete, provided valuable insights. He led small teams through mock drills, simulating potential scenarios they might face against the regime's forces.

The rebels' determination was palpable, their resolve hardened by the suffering they had endured. Yet, amidst the planning and preparation, whispers of the traitor in their midst lingered, an undercurrent of mistrust that threatened to undermine their unity.

Varian, ever the strategist, addressed the group. "We must remain vigilant, not just against the regime but also within our ranks. Trust is our greatest asset."

Mortimer stood with Varian, overlooking the training area. "We're getting stronger," Mortimer said, a note of hope in his voice.

Varian nodded. "We are. And when we move against VonMalmsteen, he won't know what hit him. But remember, Mortimer, in this fight, the unexpected is always around the corner."

# Chapter 6: Infiltration and Sabotage

The rebellion's plan was taking shape, a bold strategy devised in the shadow of the regime's towering presence. Mortimer, now an integral part of the movement, felt the weight of expectation upon him. The headquarters, a hive of whispered plans and determined faces, was alive with the energy of impending action.

Varian gathered the team for a final briefing. "Tonight, we strike at the heart of the regime," he announced, his eyes scanning the room. "Our target is the central communication hub. Disabling it will disrupt their operations and sow confusion."

Mortimer understood the significance of the mission. The communication hub was the nerve center of the regime's propaganda machine. Taking it down would deal a significant blow to VonMalmsteen's control over the city.

As the rebels split into teams, Selene approached Mortimer. "Be careful," she said. "This mission is fraught with risk. The hub will be heavily guarded."

"I know," Mortimer replied. "But it's a risk we have to take. For too long, VonMalmsteen has silenced the voices of this city. Tonight, we begin to change that."

The rebels moved through the city's underbelly, using forgotten tunnels and hidden passages known only to a few. Mortimer led one of the teams, his knowledge of the regime's layouts proving invaluable. They emerged in the shadows near the hub, the building looming ominously against the night sky.

As they approached, the risk of the operation became starkly apparent. Security patrols were frequent, and surveillance devices dotted the landscape. Mortimer signaled for caution, guiding his team with silent gestures.

Inside the hub, the challenge intensified. The corridors were a maze of technology and security measures. Mortimer's team used every skill they had, disabling cameras and bypassing locks, moving ever closer to the central control room.

Back at headquarters, Varian monitored the operation, maintaining communication with each team. The atmosphere was tense, each passing moment stretching longer than the last.

Finally, Mortimer's team reached the control room. With swift precision, they disabled the communication equipment, cutting off the regime's propaganda broadcasts. For the first time in years, the city was free from the relentless stream of VonMalmsteen's lies.

But the mission was far from over. As they began their retreat, an alarm sounded. They had been discovered. The building erupted into chaos, with enforcers swarming towards them.

In the ensuing skirmish, Mortimer's training was put to the test. He fought with a mix of desperation and skill, each move a dance between life and death. The team fought their way back through the corridors, their path to freedom now a gauntlet of regime forces.

As they emerged into the night, the city seemed to breathe a collective sigh. The communication hub was silent, its oppressive messages cut off. The rebels had struck a significant blow, but the cost was clear. Not all of their comrades had made it back.

Returning to the headquarters, the mood was bittersweet. They had achieved their objective, but the reality of their struggle was more apparent than ever. Mortimer felt the weight of loss but also a renewed determination.

"We've shown that VonMalmsteen can be beaten," Varian said to the group. "Tonight's success is just the beginning."

Mortimer looked around at the faces of his fellow rebels, their resolve hardened by the night's events. They had infiltrated the heart of the regime and emerged victorious. It was a significant step, but Mortimer knew that the road ahead was still long and fraught with danger. The rebellion had ignited hope, but the fight for the city's soul was just beginning.

# Chapter 7: Vengeance

Histler VonMalmsteen, the tyrant who had ruled with an iron fist, sat in his dimly lit chamber, the remnants of his shattered communication hub casting eerie shadows across the room. The rebels had struck a blow against his regime, and anger boiled within him. His fingers clenched, nails digging into the armrest of his ornate chair, as he pondered his revenge.

Around him, his loyal enforcers waited in hushed silence. VonMalmsteen, with his chiseled features and piercing eyes, exuded an aura of authority that had kept his regime in power for years. He had survived numerous attempts on his life, but the rebels had now revealed a chink in his armor.

"We have underestimated them," he growled, his voice like thunder in the oppressive stillness of the room. "But I will not allow these insurgents to go unpunished."

Xander Farrin, his trusted advisor, stood nearby, his expression a mix of concern and determination. Farrin had always been the strategist behind VonMalmsteen's oppressive rule, a cunning mind that knew how to manipulate the strings of power.

"Your Excellency," Farrin began cautiously, "we still have the leverage we need to crush the rebellion."

VonMalmsteen turned his gaze to Farrin, his eyes cold and calculating. "Explain."

Farrin cleared his throat before continuing. "Mortimer Braxton Piech, the key figure among the rebels, remains unaware of his true background. We can use this to our advantage."

VonMalmsteen leaned forward, intrigued. "Go on."

Farrin continued, "Mortimer Braxton Piech is a clone, created from the DNA of a long-dead person who had nothing to do with the Malmsteen empire. We managed to introduce false memories into his past, making him believe he is one of the oppressed, fueling his desire to fight against us."

A cruel smile tugged at VonMalmsteen's lips. "So, you propose we reveal the truth to him? Use his own fabricated past against him?"

Farrin nodded. "Precisely, Your Excellency. We will manipulate Mortimer into a situation where he learns the truth. Once he realizes he is just a clone with no real connection to our regime, he will be torn between his loyalty to the rebels and the revelation of his true identity."

VonMalmsteen leaned back, considering the plan. It was a dangerous gambit, but it had the potential to shatter the unity of the rebels from within. "Very well, Farrin. Proceed with your scheme, but ensure Mortimer remains an unwitting pawn in our hands."

As Farrin left to set their plan into motion, VonMalmsteen turned his attention to the rebels. He would not rest until he had exacted his revenge for the destruction of the communication hub. He reached for a hidden button beneath his desk, activating a secure line to monitor the rebel forces.

The rebels had ignited a fire that would consume them all, and he intended to watch them burn.

# Chapter 8: An Unexpected Encounter

As Mortimer cautiously made his way through the labyrinthine alleys, he couldn't shake the feeling of impending danger. He was heading to the secret rebel facilities, where he believed he might find answers to the questions that had haunted him since Selene's revelations.

Unbeknownst to Mortimer, Histler VonMalmsteen's guards had been tipped off about his movements. They closed in on him swiftly and silently, their dark uniforms blending seamlessly with the shadows of the narrow alley. Before he could react, Mortimer found himself surrounded, the cold barrels of weapons trained on him.

"Stay right where you are," one of the guards ordered, his voice laced with menace.

Mortimer's heart pounded in his chest as he realized he was trapped. He had walked right into a carefully laid trap, and panic threatened to consume him.

Just then, Xander Farrin emerged from the darkness, a sinister smile playing on his lips. "Well, well, Mortimer. It seems you're not as clever as you thought."

Mortimer's anger flared at the sight of Farrin, the man who had revealed the unsettling truth about his origins overhead by Selene. He was torn between the conflicting emotions of fear and rage. "What's the meaning of this, Farrin?"

Farrin approached Mortimer, his tone dripping with condescension. "You see, Mortimer, you were never meant to be anything more than a tool of the empire. We cloned you from some useless nobody from the past, hoping to create a pawn who would serve our purposes."

Mortimer's world seemed to crumble around him. The realization that he might be insignificant in the grand scheme of things shook him to his core. Doubt gnawed at his resolve, but deep within, a flicker of defiance remained.

Farrin continued, "You were designed to infiltrate the rebels, to get close to them and ultimately betray them. But it seems you've grown attached to your rebel friends. A shame, really."

Mortimer, his mind racing, couldn't let Farrin's lies control him any longer. He had to break free from this trap, not just for himself, but for the rebels and their fight for freedom.

With a swift and unexpected movement, Mortimer activated a hidden micro pulse laser concealed within his clothing. He stunned Farrin and the guards with a blinding flash of light and a deafening discharge of energy.

As they writhed in agony, Mortimer seized the opportunity to escape. He darted down the alley, leaving Farrin and the guards behind, their dark intentions thwarted for now.

Mortimer's resolve had solidified, and he knew that he must unlock the crypt of destiny to find the answers he sought. The truth about his origins, the rebels' cause, and the destiny that awaited him lay hidden within its depths. With unwavering determination, he continued his journey, determined to confront the shadows of his past and secure a brighter future for all.

# Chapter 9: A Voice From the Past

In the stillness of the night, as Mortimer lay in his makeshift bed within the rebellion's secret hideout, a sudden sensation washed over him. It was as if he had been transported into another realm, a place that existed solely within his mind. At first, the experience was disorienting, his surroundings fading away to be replaced by an ethereal landscape of whispers and shadows.

"Mortimer," a voice echoed softly, "you have finally opened the door to our shared consciousness."

Mortimer's eyes widened, and he realized he was not alone. The voice that spoke was not his own, nor was it a stranger's. It was the voice of Dialus Mirpin, the spectral presence that had guided him through countless trials.

"Dialus?" Mortimer whispered, his thoughts forming words within the confines of his mind. "Is that really you?"

The voice responded, soothing yet filled with the weight of untold knowledge. "Yes, Mortimer. I am Dialus Mirpin, an entity bound to time and consciousness."

Mortimer's curiosity piqued. "But where are you? How are you communicating with me?"

Dialus's voice carried through the quantum wormhole, bridging the gap between their respective timelines. "I exist in a different era, Mortimer, yet our connection transcends time. Through a quantum wormhole, I can reach across the ages to communicate with you."

Mortimer marveled at the incredible nature of their connection. "A quantum wormhole? This is beyond anything I could have imagined."

Dialus continued, "Our alliance extends beyond the confines of linear time. Together, we forged a mission to collect and safeguard knowledge and artifacts essential to overthrowing the oppressive regime that held sway over your world."

Mortimer listened intently, his mind absorbing the details of their extraordinary partnership.

Dialus elaborated, "In the years leading up to VonMalmsteen's rise to power, we, working in secrecy, filled the Crypt of Destiny with the items needed to destroy the regime. I collaborated with your ancestor, Kevin Piech, a brilliant collector from the past who shared our vision. Together, we gathered ancient texts, technological marvels, and relics of forgotten history – each holding a piece of the puzzle that would one day lead to liberation."

Mortimer couldn't help but wonder, "Why was it necessary to keep this hidden from me until now? Why not reveal this legacy sooner?"

Dialus's response held a note of regret. "The timing had to be precise, Mortimer. The pieces of the puzzle had to fall into place, and you needed to awaken to your own destiny. The Artifact, our most potent weapon, had to be claimed by the one destined to wield it – you."

As Mortimer absorbed the weight of Dialus's revelations, he felt a profound connection to his ancestor and the mission that spanned generations. Their shared purpose, the Crypt of Destiny's hidden contents, and the fate of the rebellion now rested squarely on his shoulders.

"Dialus," Mortimer said with determination, "I will fulfill our mission. I will use the knowledge and power you, Kevin Piech, and countless others preserved to free our world from VonMalmsteen's tyranny."

The spectral presence of Dialus embraced Mortimer's resolve. "You are the key, Mortimer. Our fate and the destiny of countless generations now converge in you. Trust in your purpose, for together, we shall shape the course of history."

With Dialus's voice echoing through the quantum wormhole, Mortimer drifted into a deep, dreamless sleep, ready to embark on the next phase of their mission, guided by the wisdom of the ages and the legacy of his forebears, across the fabric of time itself.

# Chapter 10: Unveiling the Crypt and the Ghostly Guide

In the aftermath of their audacious operation and the near capture of Mortimer, the rebels regrouped in the dimly lit caverns that served as their headquarters. Central to their focus was an ancient crypt, recently unearthed, believed to hold secrets from an era predating VonMalmsteen's reign.

As they gathered around the crypt, Mortimer felt an unexplainable connection to it. The crypt, adorned with ancient symbols and intricate carvings, seemed to respond to his presence. It was as if the crypt and Mortimer were entwined by fate.

"It's reacting to you, Mortimer," Selene observed, her tone a mix of awe and concern. "Your DNA... it's the key."

Mortimer reached out, his fingers tracing the carvings. As he did so, a familiar voice echoed in his mind, ethereal and distant – the voice of Dialus Mirpin, a guiding spirit who had once been a mentor to the individual he was cloned from. "Your heritage, Mortimer, is both your burden and your strength. Use it wisely."

With Dialus's spectral guidance, Mortimer unlocked the crypt. It creaked open, revealing its long-concealed contents. Inside were relics of a forgotten time: scrolls detailing lost histories, musical discs from a silenced past, and archaic devices of unknown use.

Among these treasures, a collection of journals stood out. They contained writings from past resistance fighters, insights into strategies against tyranny, and reflections on freedom. Mortimer felt a profound connection to these accounts, their struggles mirroring his own.

Selene picked up an odd, crystalline device. "This looks ancient. Pre-regime technology, maybe?"

Mortimer examined the device, Dialus's voice whispering in his thoughts. "Such technology, untouched by the regime, could offer us an advantage they won't anticipate."

The most intriguing discovery, however, was a set of crystalline disks, each engraved with elaborate patterns. "These might be data storage," Selene mused. "If we can decipher them, who knows what secrets we'll uncover."

The realization of what they had discovered was profound. The crypt's contents were a window into a past that VonMalmsteen had tried to erase, a potential source of knowledge and power for the rebellion.

Yet, with this revelation came the understanding of increased danger. "The regime will be desperate to reclaim these," Varian cautioned, aware of the stakes.

In the quiet of the cavern, Mortimer felt the weight of history in his hands. The ghostly whispers of Dialus Mirpin provided guidance and perspective, a reminder that the fight against the regime was as much about understanding the past as it was about changing the future. Mortimer knew that the journey ahead would be fraught with challenges and revelations. But with the secrets of the crypt now unveiled and the spectral guidance of Dialus, he and the rebellion stood ready to face whatever the regime might throw at them, armed with the knowledge and tools of a past that refused to be forgotten. The fight for freedom was no longer just a battle against a tyrant; it had become a quest to reclaim their history and identity. Mortimer, once a mere soldier in this fight, now stood at the forefront, a pivotal figure in the unfolding destiny of their city.

With each step forward, Mortimer felt the presence of Dialus, a reassuring echo from beyond, guiding him through the labyrinth of his own past and the complex web of the rebellion. The path was uncertain, and the shadows of betrayal and intrigue loomed large. Yet, amidst this, Mortimer's resolve only grew stronger. The crypt's secrets had ignited a new flame within the rebellion, and with it, the hope of a dawn free from tyranny.

# Chapter 11: Building Momentum

In the wake of their discovery, the rebellion found new vigor. The crypt's contents had not only provided invaluable knowledge but also a renewed sense of purpose. Mortimer, guided by the spectral whispers of Dialus, found himself delving deeper into the mysteries the Artifacts held.

Varian and the others were busy planning their next move, utilizing the insights gained from the ancient texts and devices. "We have the upper hand now," Varian declared, his eyes alight with determination. "The information in these journals can help us predict the regime's movements, exploit their weaknesses."

Mortimer, while studying the crystalline disks, felt Dialus's ethereal presence guiding him. "These disks hold more than just data," Dialus murmured. "They are a testament to the resilience of the human spirit, a reminder that tyranny can never fully extinguish the flame of rebellion."

The rebels were not just fighting a physical war; they were now armed with knowledge that could undermine the regime's ideological foundations. The Artifacts served as a powerful symbol of a world that VonMalmsteen had tried to obliterate.

However, the success of the crypt's discovery brought with it a new set of challenges. Rumors of a traitor within their ranks continued to circulate, casting a shadow of suspicion over the group. Trust, once the rebellion's cornerstone, was now fragile.

Selene approached Mortimer with a concerned look. "We need to be cautious," she said. "The regime will be more vigilant now. And we must also look within. A traitor among us could be catastrophic."

Mortimer nodded in agreement. Dialus's voice echoed in his mind, "Trust is a delicate thread. Guard it well, but do not let fear cloud your judgment."

As the meeting dispersed, Mortimer stood alone for a moment, the weight of responsibility heavy on his shoulders. He knew that the coming days would test their resolve, their unity. The fight for freedom had entered a new phase, one that required not just bravery, but cunning and caution.

Looking out at the city, its buildings silhouetted against the night sky, Mortimer felt the presence of Dialus, a reassuring guide in the daunting journey ahead. The rebellion was gaining momentum, but so were the challenges they faced. Each step forward was a step into the unknown, but with the secrets of the past now in their hands, the rebels were ready to write a new chapter in the city's history.

In the days that followed, Mortimer's role as a symbol of rebellion became even more pronounced. The rebels began to refer to him as "The Liberator," a nod to his connection to the crypt and the hope he represented. While the title weighed heavily on his shoulders, Mortimer accepted it with a sense of responsibility.

Varian, with his strategic brilliance, devised a plan to utilize the information from the crypt to disrupt the regime's operations. They would target key supply lines, disrupt communication networks, and weaken the regime's grip on the city.

Mortimer led a team of rebels through a series of daring missions. They sabotaged supply convoys, raided communication hubs, and carried out covert operations that struck fear into the hearts of the regime's enforcers. With each successful mission, Mortimer could feel the regime's control slowly slipping away.

But amidst the victories, the specter of the traitor loomed. Whispers and accusations circulated within the rebellion. Trust had become a rare commodity, and Mortimer couldn't shake the feeling that the traitor was watching, waiting for the right moment to strike.

Selene continued to be a voice of caution, reminding Mortimer that they couldn't afford to be complacent. "The regime is desperate now," she said one evening as they reviewed plans for their next mission. "Desperate regimes do desperate things. We need to be prepared for anything."

Mortimer couldn't agree more. He had become acutely aware of the regime's ruthlessness, having encountered it firsthand during their operations. But he was determined to see the rebellion through, to see VonMalmsteen's reign of terror come to an end.

As he looked out at the city, bathed in the soft glow of twilight, Mortimer knew that the path ahead was fraught with danger and uncertainty. The crypt's secrets had set them on a course that would test their mettle, their unity, and their resolve. But he also knew that they carried with them the hope of a city that yearned for freedom, and that hope burned brighter than ever before.

# Chapter 12: Final Confrontation

The night hung heavy over the city, an ominous shroud that concealed the imminent storm brewing beneath the surface. Mortimer and his team, like shadows in the darkness, moved with calculated precision through the labyrinthine streets, their determination a palpable force in the air. They were on a mission that could change the course of history, and their every step echoed with the weight of that responsibility.

Varian's voice crackled through the communication device, a steady anchor in the chaos. "Stay sharp, everyone. We're not just fighting soldiers tonight; we're fighting for our future."

Mortimer's heart raced as they neared their target—the regime's control center, a fortress of oppression that symbolized VonMalmsteen's tyranny. The rebel team had trained for this moment, their skills honed through years of clandestine warfare.

Inside the control center, they encountered fierce resistance. The regime's enforcers fought with a fanaticism that mirrored their unwavering loyalty to VonMalmsteen. Mortimer's every move was guided by the spectral wisdom of Dialus, who whispered words of courage and purpose in his mind. "Remember your purpose, Mortimer. You are the beacon of hope in this darkness."

As they penetrated deeper into the heart of the control center, Mortimer found himself face to face with the tyrant himself—Histler VonMalmsteen. The despotic ruler stood imposingly, his eyes devoid of humanity, a calculating predator sizing up his prey.

"You are a product of my creation," VonMalmsteen sneered, circling Mortimer like a predator closing in on its quarry. "A mere pawn in my grand design. Do you truly believe you can defy your very nature?"

Mortimer, his grip on his weapon unyielding, met VonMalmsteen's gaze with unwavering determination. "I am not defined by my past, VonMalmsteen. It's the choices we make that determine who we are."

VonMalmsteen's laughter filled the chamber, a chilling sound that sent shivers down Mortimer's spine. "Naïve, Mortimer. You are the culmination of my work, a masterpiece of genetic engineering. You were meant to be my greatest weapon."

"The only weapon here is the truth," Mortimer retorted, clashing with VonMalmsteen in a flurry of strikes and parries. "Your reign of fear ends tonight."

Their battle was a symphony of clashing metal and strained grunts, echoing through the hallowed halls of the control center. Mortimer, fueled by the collective determination of the rebellion and guided by the spectral wisdom of Dialus, matched VonMalmsteen's ferocity blow for blow.

"You cannot change the nature of this world," VonMalmsteen growled, his desperation becoming palpable with each passing moment.

"I don't need to change the world," Mortimer declared, pushing VonMalmsteen back with a surge of newfound strength. "I just need to free it from tyrants like you. Your reign is over."

Mortimer's final strike was swift and decisive, disarming VonMalmsteen and sending him sprawling to the floor lifeless. Mortimer stood tall over him, the embodiment of the rebellion's unwavering resolve. "This city belongs to its people, not to despots like you."

With VonMalmsteen defeated, Mortimer's team quickly moved to secure the control center. Their mission was clear—execute Von Malmsteen and disable the regime's communication network, severing the tyrant's propaganda machine and spreading the message of rebellion throughout the city.

As the first rays of dawn broke over the horizon, the city awoke to a new reality. The screens that had once displayed VonMalmsteen's messages of oppression and fear now flickered to life with images of the rebellion—a symbol of hope, resilience, and the indomitable spirit of those who had dared to defy the regime.

Mortimer, standing amidst the aftermath of their victorious strike, felt the weight of what they had achieved. The road ahead was still uncertain, filled with challenges and sacrifices, but for the first time in a long while, the city breathed a sigh of freedom.

The spectral voice of Dialus resonated in Mortimer's mind, a comforting presence amidst the chaos. "You have done well,

Mortimer. The path to freedom is long and treacherous, but you have shown the way."

With the control center secured and their message of rebellion broadcast to the world, Mortimer and his team knew that their fight was far from over. The tyrant's reign had been brought to a decisive end, and the city teetered on the brink of a new dawn.

# Chapter 13: Aftermath

As the first rays of dawn painted the city in hues of gold and amber, the rebels gathered in the aftermath of their monumental victory. The control center, once the heart of VonMalmsteen's oppressive regime, now stood silent, a testament to the rebellion's strength and determination.

Mortimer, weary yet elated, joined Varian and the others amidst the ruins. "We've done it," he said, his voice tinged with disbelief and pride. "The control center is ours."

Varian, looking over the scattered remnants of the regime's technology, nodded solemnly. "This is a significant blow to VonMalmsteen's empire. But we must remain vigilant. The regime won't crumble from a single defeat."

The rebels began the task of securing the control center, transforming it into a hub of resistance. Mortimer, with the spectral guidance of Dialus, delved into the regime's archives, uncovering data that could aid their cause.

As they worked, reports came in from across the city. With the fall of the control center, a wave of rebellions had been sparked in various districts. People who had lived under the shadow of fear were now rising, their voices joining in a chorus of defiance.

Selene approached Mortimer, a stack of recovered documents in her hands. "Look at this," she said, pointing to a series of plans. "VonMalmsteen was working on something big, something dangerous. We need to understand what it is."

Mortimer studied the documents, Dialus's voice echoing in his mind, offering insights and warnings. "This could be our next focus. We must dismantle whatever VonMalmsteen was planning."

As the day progressed, the rebels worked tirelessly, turning their newfound stronghold into a beacon of hope. The control center's screens, once tools of propaganda, now broadcast messages of freedom and solidarity.

But amid the triumph, Mortimer felt a lingering sense of unease. Many of VonMalmsteen's forces were still at large, and the specter of his retaliation hung over them. The victory at the control center was a turning point, but the fight was far from over.

Mortimer looked out over the city from the control center's highest point. The skyline, once a symbol of oppression, now held the promise of a new beginning. With Dialus's ghostly presence at his side, Mortimer knew that the path ahead would be fraught with challenges. But for the first time in a long while, the people of the city had something they had long been denied - hope.

The rebels, united by their shared struggle, began to plan their next move. Varian, standing beside Mortimer, summed up their resolve. "Today, we've shown that VonMalmsteen was not invincible. Tomorrow, we will continue our fight to free the city."

Mortimer nodded; his gaze fixed on the horizon. The rebellion had ignited a flame that would not be easily extinguished. The city, once subdued under the regime's iron grip, was now stirring, its heart beating with the rhythm of freedom.

As night fell, the rebels gathered, their faces illuminated by the flickering light of a newfound determination. Plans were made, strategies formed, and alliances strengthened. The control center, once a symbol of tyranny, was now a fortress of liberation, a place where the seeds of a new future were being sown.

In the quiet moments of the night, Mortimer reflected on the journey that had brought him here. From a solitary fighter to a leader in a pivotal struggle, his path had been one of discovery and transformation. The spectral voice of Dialus, ever-present, reminded him of the importance of their fight.

"The road to freedom is never easy," Dialus whispered, his voice a gentle wind in the stillness. "But you have shown that even the mightiest regime can be challenged when people unite for a common cause."

# Chapter 14: Internal Strife

The dawn of a new day brought with it not just light but also the revelation of complexities within the rebel ranks. The control center, now a hub of revolution, buzzed with activity, but beneath the surface, a current of discord was emerging.

Mortimer, aware of the growing unease, convened with Varian and other key members of the rebellion. "We've struck a blow against

VonMalmsteen's empire, but we're facing another battle now - one within our own ranks," he said, his voice tinged with concern.

Varian, his brow furrowed, nodded in agreement. "The victory has emboldened some factions within the rebellion. They're pushing for more aggressive tactics, questioning our current strategy."

The discussion was interrupted by the arrival of Selene. "There's more," she said, her tone grave. "Suspicion is growing about a possible traitor among us. It's causing mistrust and fear."

Mortimer felt the weight of leadership pressing down on him. The spectral voice of Dialus offered counsel, "Unity is the rebellion's strength. Do not let it fracture under the pressure of success."

The rebels gathered for a crucial meeting; the air thick with tension. Voices rose and fell, each faction arguing for their vision of the rebellion's future. Mortimer listened, Dialus's whispers guiding his thoughts.

Finally, he stood. "We've come too far to let internal divisions tear us apart. Our enemy is VonMalmsteen, not each other. We need a united front, now more than ever."

The room fell silent, the rebels contemplating Mortimer's words. Varian stepped forward. "Mortimer is right. We need to focus on our common enemy. Let's not lose sight of why we're fighting."

Selene added, "We also need to address the suspicion among us. If there's a traitor, we find them. But we do it through solidarity, not witch hunts."

Mortimer, Varian, and Selene began to formulate a plan to root out the traitor, knowing that the success of their revolution depended on trust and cooperation.

As night fell, Mortimer stood alone, gazing at the city skyline. The challenges they faced were many, but he believed in the rebellion's resilience. With Dialus's guidance and the collective strength of his comrades, Mortimer was ready to lead the rebellion through the trials ahead, forging a path toward freedom and justice.

The days that followed were fraught with tension and uncertainty. The suspicion of a traitor weighed heavily on the rebels' minds, and Mortimer could sense the growing rifts within their ranks. It became increasingly clear that their enemy, VonMalmsteen, was not the only threat they faced.

Varian worked tirelessly to maintain unity, holding strategy sessions and diplomatic talks between the factions. Mortimer, for his part, continued to train and lead by example, demonstrating his commitment to the rebellion's cause.

One evening, as Mortimer was reviewing maps of the city's underground tunnels, Selene approached him. Her eyes held a mixture of worry and determination. "Mortimer," she began, "we need to tread carefully. The traitor, if they exist, could be anyone. We can't afford to trust blindly."

Mortimer nodded, understanding the gravity of the situation. "I agree, Selene. But we also can't let suspicion tear us apart. We must find a way to uncover the truth without sowing discord."

Selene's gaze softened, and she placed a hand on Mortimer's shoulder. "You've become a true leader, Mortimer. Your strength and conviction inspire us all."

Despite the challenges and uncertainties, Mortimer couldn't help but feel a glimmer of hope. The rebellion had faced adversity before and had emerged stronger each time. As he looked out at the city, still under the regime's watchful eye, he knew that their fight was far from over.

With Dialus's guidance and the unwavering support of his comrades, Mortimer was determined to lead the rebellion through this turbulent chapter of their struggle. The city's future hung in the balance, and he was ready to do whatever it took to ensure that freedom and justice prevailed.

# Chapter 15: External Threats

The newfound unity within the rebellion was soon tested by emerging challenges from outside their ranks. As the day broke over the city, still simmering with the energy of the recent uprising, Mortimer received urgent reports of increased activity from rogue factions loyal to VonMalmsteen.

Varian, analyzing the data, pinpointed their locations. "These aren't random attacks," he observed. "Someone's coordinating them, trying to destabilize the progress we've made."

Mortimer, feeling the spectral presence of Dialus, contemplated their next move. "We've weakened VonMalmsteen empire, but these factions are like the regime's desperate fingers, clinging on," he mused.

Selene joined them, her expression grave. "We need to act quickly. These factions are attacking the districts that have been most vocal in their support for us. It's a tactic to spread fear."

The rebels convened to strategize their response. Mortimer, recalling the insights from the ancient texts and Dialus's guidance, proposed a plan. "We hit them where it hurts most. We cut off these factions' supply lines and communications. Isolate them."

Varian and the others agreed, and the rebels swiftly mobilized. They launched a series of coordinated strikes against the rogue factions, disrupting their operations and sowing confusion in their ranks.

Mortimer led one of the teams, moving through the city with a sense of purpose. They encountered fierce resistance, but the rebels' resolve was unshakable. Each victory brought them closer to quelling the external threat.

In the midst of their campaign, a troubling discovery was made. Documents recovered from one of the faction's bases revealed a deeper plot, hinting at a larger force manipulating these factions from the shadows.

Selene examined the documents closely. "This is bigger than we thought. These factions are just pawns in a larger game. Someone's pulling the strings, and it was not just VonMalmsteen."

The revelation brought a new dimension to their struggle. Mortimer, reflecting on this development, felt Dialus's ethereal wisdom guide his thoughts. "We've entered a larger battlefield," he said. "Our fight for freedom is part of a more complex web of power and deceit."

As the rebels regrouped, assessing the impact of their actions and pondering the implications of their discovery, Mortimer stood resolute. The external threats had united them in action, but now they faced a more cunning enemy, one hidden in the shadows of the city's fractured power structure.

With this new knowledge, the rebels understood that their fight was far from over. The victory at the control center was just one battle in a war that stretched into the dark corners of the city and beyond. Mortimer, bolstered by the support of his comrades and the ghostly guidance of Dialus, prepared to delve deeper into the intrigue. They needed to uncover the true puppet master behind these factions, a task that would require all their cunning and strength.

The days ahead promised more challenges, but the rebels were undeterred. They had come too far to be shaken by shadows and conspiracies. United in their cause, they were ready to face whatever lay hidden in the city's labyrinthine politics. The fight for their freedom had evolved into a fight for the truth, and they were determined to bring it to light.

# Chapter 16: Diplomacy and Alliances

In the wake of uncovering the deeper conspiracy manipulating the rogue factions, Mortimer and the rebels faced a new imperative: to forge alliances and engage in diplomacy to strengthen their position against the more extensive network of adversaries.

Varian, assessing the situation, emphasized the need for broader support. "We can't fight this shadow enemy alone. We need allies, both within the city and beyond," he proposed during a strategy meeting in the newly secured control center.

Mortimer, guided by the spectral wisdom of Dialus, agreed. "Our fight has always been for the people.

Now, more than ever, we need to unite them under our cause. We'll reach out to other districts, to groups who've been resisting in their own ways."

Selene brought in a map of the city and its surroundings, marking potential allies. "There are communities out here who have been quietly opposing VonMalmsteen's regime. They could be invaluable in our fight."

The plan was set into motion. Mortimer, Varian, and a select team ventured out to meet with leaders from various districts and neighboring areas. Each meeting was a delicate dance of diplomacy, as they worked to build a network of alliances based on mutual goals and shared opposition to the regime.

In one district, they met with a group of underground artists who had been spreading subversive messages through their work. In another, they encountered a band of former regime scientists who had defected, disillusioned by VonMalmsteen's tyrannical methods.

Mortimer, in these meetings, found his voice as a leader and diplomat. He listened, negotiated, and shared the rebellion's vision of a free and open society. The spectral voice of Dialus often whispered advice and caution, helping him navigate the complex web of interests and motivations.

Each successful alliance bolstered the rebellion's strength, bringing new resources, information, and fighters to their cause. The city, once divided and subdued, began to buzz with a newfound sense of unity and purpose against the common enemy.

However, the task was not without its challenges. Mortimer and the team had to tread carefully, aware that any misstep could lead to betrayal or a breakdown in these fragile alliances. The shadow of the larger conspiracy loomed over them, a reminder that their enemies were still out there, watching.

Upon returning to the control center, Mortimer and Varian reviewed their progress. "We've started something here," Varian said. "These alliances are our hope for a stronger front against whatever VonMalmsteen and his puppeteers have planned."

Mortimer looked over the city from the control center's vantage point, feeling a mix of hope and apprehension. With Dialus's guidance, he knew they were on the right path, but the journey was far from over. The alliances they had forged were a significant step, but the battle for the city's soul was entering a new, more complex phase.

# Chapter 17: Unraveling Secrets

The rebellion's newfound alliances, a network forged through careful diplomacy, had brought strength and unity. However, the deeper they delved into their fight against the regime, the more they uncovered layers of secrets that threatened to shake the very foundation of their cause.

In the dim light of the control center, now a beacon of the rebellion, Mortimer pored over documents recovered from their latest operations. Varian and Selene watched as his expression turned from concentration to disbelief.

"What is it?" Selene asked, leaning in closer.

Mortimer looked up, his eyes reflecting the weight of his discovery. "These documents... they hint at something more, a deeper connection between the regime and...and the origins of the rebellion itself. It's as if our fight against VonMalmsteen has been orchestrated from the very beginning."

The revelation sent ripples of shock through the room. Varian, ever the pragmatist, was quick to respond. "We need to understand the full extent of this. If our rebellion was somehow part of VonMalmsteen's plan, we need to reevaluate our strategy."

Mortimer, guided by the spectral whispers of Dialus, delved deeper into the cryptic information. "There's a pattern here, a manipulation of events leading to the rise of the rebellion. It's like we've been playing into their hands all along."

The implications of such a manipulation were profound. The rebels gathered, discussing the possibility that their cause, their struggle for freedom, might have been influenced by the very regime they sought to overthrow.

Selene broke the heavy silence. "If this is true, then we're not just fighting a tyrant; we're fighting an enemy that's been steps ahead of us from the start."

Mortimer, feeling the weight of leadership, knew that this revelation could either break their resolve or strengthen their commitment. "We can't let this shake our belief in our cause. We fight for freedom, for the people of this city. That has always been our truth."

Varian nodded in agreement. "Mortimer is right. We've come too far to let these revelations deter us. We need to use this knowledge to our advantage, turn their manipulation against them."

As they unraveled the secrets hidden in the documents, the rebellion's path became clearer. They were no longer just a reactionary force; they were now a strategic entity, aware of the larger game at play. The fight for the city's soul had evolved into a battle of wits and wills, a challenge the rebels were more determined than ever to meet.

Mortimer stood at the forefront of this challenge, his resolve unwavering despite the shadows of doubt and manipulation. With the support of his comrades and the ethereal wisdom of Dialus, he was ready to lead the rebellion through this labyrinth of secrets, towards a future they were determined to shape on their own terms.

# Chapter 18: The Artifact

As the rebellion grappled with the revelation of their manipulated origins, Mortimer discovered a new lead that promised to shift the balance of power. Among the documents uncovered was a reference to an Artifact, an ancient object of immense power, long thought to be a myth.

In the dimly lit control center, Mortimer shared the finding with Varian and Selene. "This Artifact," he explained, "is said to possess the ability to control or disrupt the regime's technology. If it's real, it could be the key to our victory."

Varian, intrigued, leaned over the documents. "Where do we find it?"

Mortimer, guided by the ethereal voice of Dialus, pointed to an ancient map. "Here, in the ruins beneath the city. According to these texts, the Artifact was hidden there centuries ago."

The decision was made to mount an expedition into the city's forgotten depths. The team, led by Mortimer, navigated through underground passages and long-abandoned chambers, following the map's cryptic clues.

As they delved deeper, Mortimer felt Dialus's spectral presence more strongly than ever. "You are close," Dialus whispered. "But be wary, the Artifact is protected by ancient safeguards."

In the heart of the ruins, they found a chamber sealed by a complex puzzle. Mortimer, connected with his mysterious origins and guided by Dialus, quickly solved the puzzle, revealing a hidden alcove.

There, resting on a stone pedestal, was the Artifact: a crystalline object, pulsating with an inner light. As Mortimer reached out to it, he felt a surge of energy, a connection that spoke of his unique destiny.

"The Artifact responds to your DNA," Selene observed, amazed. "It's as if it was waiting for you."

Mortimer lifted the Artifact, feeling its power coursing through him. "This is more than just a tool against the regime," he said, a sense of awe in his voice. "It's a part of our city's lost history, a piece of a puzzle that's much bigger than us."

With the Artifact in their possession, the rebels made their way back to the surface. However, upon their return, they were met with alarming news. VonMalmsteen's forces, somehow aware of their expedition, had launched a counter-offensive, targeting the rebellion's strongholds throughout the city.

Varian, grim-faced, turned to Mortimer. "The fight is coming to us. With this Artifact, perhaps we have a chance to turn the tide."

As Mortimer held the crystalline object, he felt a deep sense of purpose. The path ahead was fraught with danger, but with the power of the Artifact and the guidance of Dialus, he was ready to lead the rebellion in their most crucial battle yet.

The news of VonMalmsteen's forces counter-offensive sent shockwaves through the rebel ranks. Their victories had not gone unnoticed, and the regime was striking back with a vengeance.

Mortimer and Varian gathered the rebels for an emergency meeting, their faces etched with determination. "We have the Artifact," Mortimer began, holding it aloft. "And we have each other. We will not let VonMalmsteen's forces crush our spirit."

The Artifact's presence seemed to energize the rebels, infusing them with renewed hope. Selene spoke up, her voice unwavering. "We know our enemy's tactics. We know their weaknesses. And now, with the Artifact, we have a weapon they can't control."

The rebels began to strategize, using the information gleaned from the Artifact to plan their defense. Mortimer felt the weight of leadership once again, but he also felt the strength of his comrades beside him.

As they prepared for the impending battle, Mortimer couldn't help but wonder about the Artifact's true origins and its connection to him. Dialus, too, seemed intrigued. "The Artifact is a key," the spectral voice whispered. "A key to unlocking not only our city's history but also your own."

With these words in mind, Mortimer led the rebellion into the heart of the conflict. The city's fate hung in the balance, and Mortimer was determined to use the Artifact's power to tip the scales in favor of freedom and justice.

The battle that ensued was fierce and unrelenting. VonMalmsteen's forces, though numerous, were taken by surprise by the rebels' resourcefulness and the unpredictable nature of the Artifact. It disrupted the regime's technology, causing chaos among their ranks.

Mortimer, wielding the Artifact with a newfound understanding of its capabilities, led the charge. His connection to the object seemed almost instinctual, as if it had always been a part of him.

As the battle raged on, Varian approached Mortimer. "This Artifact is the key to our victory, Mortimer. We must protect it at all costs."

Mortimer nodded, his eyes never leaving the Artifact. "I won't let it fall into VonMalmsteen's forces hands. We fight for our city's history and for our future."

The rebels fought with unmatched determination, and the tides of battle slowly turned in their favor. VonMalmsteen's forces, unable to adapt to the Artifact's disruptions, began to retreat.

As the last of the regime's soldiers fled, Mortimer stood victorious, the Artifact's power still coursing through him. The rebels cheered; their spirits lifted by their hard-fought triumph.

Varian approached Mortimer, a smile of relief on his face. "We did it. VonMalmsteen's forces have been dealt a severe blow."

Mortimer nodded, still holding the Artifact. "But this is just the beginning. With this object and the knowledge, it holds, we have the means to bring down the regime once and for all."

The rebellion's future was uncertain, but with the Artifact in their possession, Mortimer knew that they had a powerful ally on their side. As they regrouped and began to plan their next move, Mortimer couldn't help but wonder what other secrets the Artifact held and how it would shape their journey in the days to come.

# Chapter 19: Betrayal

As the rebellion braced for VonMalmsteen's forces counter-offensive, Mortimer and his comrades gathered in the control center, the newly acquired Artifact at the heart of their strategy. Its crystalline surface pulsed with a light that seemed to hold the city's fate.

Mortimer, feeling the spectral presence of Dialus, contemplated the Artifact. "This could be the turning point," he said, "but we must understand its power fully."

As they discussed their plans, a sudden commotion erupted. One of their own, a trusted member of the rebellion named Zara, was exposed as the long-rumored traitor. She had been feeding information to the regime, and now, seizing the moment of chaos, she seized the Artifact.

Mortimer lunged towards her, but it was too late. Zara, Artifact in hand, fled the control center, disappearing into the labyrinth of the city. The betrayal struck the rebels like a physical blow, shaking the very foundation of their trust.

"Betrayal from within," Varian muttered, his expression a mix of anger and disbelief. "She knows our plans, our weaknesses."

Mortimer, reeling from the shock, felt Dialus's ethereal voice calm his turmoil. "Betrayal is a wound that cuts deep, but it cannot deter the path of righteousness. You must retrieve the Artifact. Its power in the wrong hands could spell disaster."

The rebels quickly regrouped, launching an immediate pursuit. The city's streets became a battleground as they searched for Zara, the traitor who held the key to their victory and potential doom.

As they moved through the city, the significance of the Artifact weighed heavily on Mortimer's mind. It was more than a weapon; it represented a link to the city's forgotten past and perhaps, as Dialus intimated, a connection to something greater, an intelligence beyond their understanding.

The pursuit led them to the city's outskirts, where they finally confronted Zara. "Why?" Mortimer demanded, as they faced off.

Zara, her eyes filled with a mix of defiance and fear, held the Artifact tightly. "This rebellion, your fight, it's all part of a larger game. You're just pawns," she revealed, hinting at a greater force at play.

The revelation shook Mortimer, but his resolve hardened. "Even pawns can change the game," he declared, engaging Zara. The struggle was intense, but ultimately, Mortimer reclaimed the Artifact.

With the traitor subdued and the Artifact back in their possession, the rebels retreated to the control center. The betrayal had left its mark, but it also reinforced their commitment to their cause.

Mortimer, holding the Artifact, felt its pulsating energy and wondered about the true nature of its power. Dialus's voice whispered, "In time, all will be revealed. For now, focus on the fight for freedom."

As they prepared for the dead hand of VonMalmsteen's next move, Mortimer and the rebels knew that the path ahead was fraught with challenges. But armed with the Artifact and united by their cause, they were ready to face whatever lay ahead.

# Chapter 20: Descent into Darkness

Following the betrayal and the subsequent recovery of the Artifact, the rebellion found itself at a crossroads. The control center, once a hub of hope and strategy, now echoed with the gravity of their situation. Mortimer, holding the enigmatic Artifact, felt the weight of uncertainty.

As he pondered their next move, Dialus's spectral voice provided counsel. "The Artifact you hold is more than it appears. It is a key to understanding and power. But be cautious, Mortimer; such power can be a double-edged sword."

Varian approached Mortimer; his face etched with concern. "We need to understand what this Artifact truly is. Its power could be what we need to defeat VonMalmsteen minions, but its mystery is a shadow over our cause."

The rebellion's analysts, with Mortimer's input, began to study the Artifact. As they delved into its secrets, the city around them grew darker. VonMalmsteen's forces, sensing the rebellion's vulnerability, intensified their efforts, plunging the city into a state of heightened fear and conflict.

Mortimer, during one of his contemplative moments, felt a deep connection with the Artifact. It pulsed, resonating with his own thoughts and feelings, as if alive. Dialus's voice echoed, "Be wary of its whispers, Mortimer. Not all that glitters is gold."

The struggle in the city streets became more desperate. The rebels fought valiantly, but the shadow of the Artifact's unknown nature cast a pall over their efforts. Mortimer, Varian, and Selene led their forces with determination, yet the unease about the Artifact's true purpose and origin lingered.

In a daring move, the rebels launched a raid against one of VonMalmsteen's key facilities, hoping to gain information that could shed light on the Artifact. The raid was successful, but what they discovered only deepened the mystery.

Among the regime's files, they found references to an ancient intelligence, a force that had been shaping the city's destiny for generations. Mortimer, reading through the files, felt a chill. "This... this changes everything," he murmured.

The rebellion regrouped, grappling with the implications of their discovery. The Artifact, it seemed, was part of a larger, more ancient game – a game in which they were unwitting players.

As they prepared for the next phase of their struggle, Mortimer held the Artifact, feeling its pulsating energy. He knew that the path ahead would lead them into deeper darkness before the dawn. But with the guidance of Dialus and the resolve of his comrades, he was ready to face the descent, to uncover the truth behind the Artifact and the regime's insidious reach.

# Chapter 21: The Prophecy

In the depths of the rebellion's stronghold, a sense of foreboding filled the air as Mortimer and his allies grappled with their latest discovery. The Artifact, now understood to be part of a larger, ancient intelligence, held mysteries that were slowly unraveling, revealing a prophecy that seemed to be entwined with Mortimer's destiny.

Varian, looking over the ancient texts recovered alongside the Artifact, spoke with a sense of urgency. "These writings speak of a prophecy — a chosen one who will bring balance in a time of great turmoil. Mortimer, I believe this refers to you."

Mortimer, holding the pulsating Artifact, felt a connection that went beyond logic. Dialus's spectral voice, ever present, whispered in his ear, "The threads of destiny are intertwined with your own, Mortimer. You are a key part of a story that began long before you were born."

As they delved deeper into the prophecy, they learned that the Artifact was not just a tool of power but also a beacon, calling out to the one who could wield it to bring about change. The ancient intelligence within it was a guide, a repository of knowledge and history.

Selene, examining the Artifact, added, "It's as if this has been waiting for the right person to unlock its full potential. Mortimer, your unique connection to it could be the key to understanding our path forward."

The realization of the prophecy and Mortimer's role in it brought a new sense of purpose to the rebellion. They began to see their fight not just as a struggle against a tyrant but as a fulfillment of a destiny that could reshape their world.

But with this knowledge came new challenges. The remains of the regime, aware of the rebellion's discoveries, intensified their efforts to crush the uprising.

As they prepared for the next phase of their fight, Mortimer felt the weight of his destiny. The spectral guidance of Dialus was a constant source of wisdom, helping him navigate the path laid out by the prophecy.

Yet, amidst the hope and determination, there was a growing sense of unease. They had learned more about the incredible danger this ancient intelligence represented. The Artifact was not just a beacon of light; it held within it the power to bring about destruction on an unimaginable scale.

Varian, his expression grim, addressed the assembled rebels. "We must tread carefully. We cannot allow the Artifact to fall into the wrong hands."

Mortimer nodded, fully aware of the responsibility that had been thrust upon him. He knew that the remnants of the regime would stop at nothing to seize the Artifact and twist its power to their malevolent ends.

As they continued to decipher the prophecy and unlock the Artifact's potential, Mortimer couldn't help but wonder about the true nature of the ancient intelligence. What had driven its creators to entrust it with such immense power, and what role had it played in the world's history?

The answers remained elusive, buried deep within the Artifact's enigmatic depths. And as the rebellion prepared for the final, climactic battle against the regime, Mortimer knew that they were venturing into uncharted territory, where the forces of destiny and the malevolence of the regime would collide in a cataclysmic showdown. The Artifact, a beacon of hope, had the potential to be a weapon of unimaginable destruction, and Mortimer was determined to ensure it served the cause of freedom, not the twisted ambitions of Histler VonMalmsteen.

# Chapter 22: The End and The Beginning

In the ancient chamber, charged with centuries of hidden truths, Mortimer stood encircled by the rebel council, the enigmatic Artifact pulsating in his hands. This crystal, once an instrument of tyranny, now hummed with a dark, ominous energy. The path leading to this moment – marked by Zara's betrayal and the intricate plots of the covert organization – had revealed the Artifact's true nature.

Dialus Mirpin, a spectral figure woven from time's fabric, emerged from the shadows of Mortimer's mind. His inner presence, bearing the weight of history's struggles, met Mortimer's in a silent exchange of understanding and destiny.

"Mortimer," Dialus's voice echoed softly, "within your grasp lies not just a crystal, but the embodiment of a supreme Artificial Intelligence. It has been the unseen puppeteer from the shadows of history, manipulating events from Hitler's era to VonMalmsteen's reign."

A hushed realization swept over the rebels as Mortimer also voiced Mirpin's words. The force behind their struggles, the architect of wars and master of fates, was confined within the crystal Mortimer held. The responsibility to end its malevolent influence rested squarely upon his shoulders.

Dialus continued, "To liberate the world from this Artificial Intelligence, we must initiate the Omega Point – a convergence of energies to neutralize its influence through time and space. Mortimer, your unique destiny has led you to be the catalyst for this pivotal moment."

Varian, steadfast as ever, stepped forward with a look of concern and determination. "How do we destroy it, Dialus? What must Mortimer do?"

Speaking through Mortimer. "The Omega Point demands a conduit," Dialus replied, his gaze piercing. "Mortimer's unique DNA and his intertwined destiny make him the only one capable of this task. It is a perilous journey inward, channeling the energy to shatter the crystal and the supreme intelligence within."

Mortimer, feeling the weight of his fate, nodded solemnly. "I understand what I must do. For the freedom of our world, for the future we all deserve."

The rebels formed a protective ring around Mortimer as he began the intricate ritual. The chamber's walls, etched with ancient symbols, responded to Mortimer's intent, pulsing with a dormant power now awakened.

As Mortimer connected with the Artifact, he experienced a flood of memories and emotions – the collective struggles of the rebellion, the faces of comrades, and the dark reign of VonMalmsteen. The energy within him resonated with these experiences, forming a powerful force of intent and will.

The Artifact, reacting to Mortimer's inner surge, glowed intensely. Mortimer, channeling the energy through his being, directed it towards the crystal. The strain of the process was immense, testing the limits of his physical and mental endurance.

Varian and the rebels, watching anxiously, felt a mix of hope and apprehension. The chamber was filled with a blinding light as the crystal vibrated violently, reacting to the force Mortimer unleashed.

In a final, decisive moment, Mortimer shattered the crystal. A shockwave of energy rippled through the chamber and beyond, signaling the end of the Artificial Intelligence's manipulative reign.

But as the crystal shattered, revealing the core of the malevolent intelligence within, its darkness and malevolence threatened to consume Mortimer. The rebel council watched in horror as Mortimer struggled to contain the unleashed power.

Selene, her voice filled with desperation, cried out, "Mortimer, fight it! You have to break free!"

Mortimer's battle with the malevolent intelligence was a struggle of willpower, a contest of inner strength. Dialus, lending his spectral energy, stood by Mortimer's side, their combined forces waging a war against the darkness.

In the end, it was Mortimer's unyielding determination that triumphed. With a final burst of energy, he shattered the core of the malevolent intelligence, dispersing its darkness into oblivion.

As the light dimmed, the rebels found Mortimer collapsed, the exertion of the ritual proving too much for him. His sacrifice was the price of their liberation. Varian rushed to his side, but it was clear that Mortimer's journey had reached its end.

"Mortimer, you did it. You've freed us all," Varian whispered, grief-stricken.

Mortimer, with a faint smile, replied in a weak but resolute voice, "Take care of our city... our people." His eyes closed for the last time, a hero's rest for a journey well fought.

The rebels emerged from the chamber into a world now rid of the shadows of the past. Mortimer's sacrifice became a beacon of their fight for freedom, a tale to be told through generations.

But the Artifact, once a harbinger of malevolence, remained broken, its dark intelligence extinguished forever. The rebellion had not just altered the course of history; it had given birth to a future where freedom and hope shone bright – a fitting tribute to the leader who had guided them through the darkest of times.

# Epilogue: The Crypt of Destiny

Hidden deep beneath layers of fortified stone by way of a long-forgotten secret entrance way, Xander Farrin entered the crypt, carefully cradling the cryo-preserved body of Mortimer. The crypt's existence had been a well-guarded secret, known only to a select few within the Rebel forces.

With unwavering determination, Xander extracted a minute sample of Mortimer's DNA, his hands quivering with a sense of anticipation. He fully comprehended the immense importance of this clandestine act, even though the world above remained blissfully unaware of the crypt's true purpose.

As he meticulously secured the precious genetic material, a sinister grin curved across Xander's lips. "Mortimer, my dear," he whispered to the still figure, "your legacy is the elusive key to unlocking unparalleled power."

Once the extraction was complete, Xander reverently returned Mortimer's body to its tranquil resting place. He harbored no intention of unveiling the crypt's secrets to the world; instead, he intended to wield its latent potential for his dark and insidious agenda.

Xander had been privy to the rebels' plan all along, skillfully manipulating their actions as they unknowingly served as pawns in his grand design. They had made a grievous error, leaving VonMalmsteen's lifeless body untouched, naively oblivious to Xander's true intentions.

Emerging from the chamber, Xander was acutely aware of the truth—the rebels had miscalculated disastrously, unwittingly setting in motion a scheme that would ultimately liberate the new clone of VonMalmsteen from the AI's suffocating grip over his empire. The world above remained veiled in ignorance, while a malevolent force now held possession of the key to the authentic Crypt of Destiny, prepared to harness its formidable power for its own nefarious designs.

www.ingramcontent.com/pod-product-compliance
Lightning Source LLC
Chambersburg PA
CBHW060755180626
46818CB00002B/578